THE ZACK FILES™

Never Trust a Cat Who Wears Earrings

For Judith, and for the real Zack,
with love—D.G.

Never Trust a Cat Who Wears Earrings

By Dan Greenburg

Illustrated by Jack E. Davis

GROSSET & DUNLAP • NEW YORK

I'd like to thank my editors,
Jane O'Connor and Judy Donnelly,
who make the process of writing and revising
so much fun, and without whom
these books would not exist.

I also want to thank
Jennifer Dussling and Laura Driscoll
for their terrific ideas.

Text copyright © 1997 by Dan Greenburg. Illustrations copyright © 1997 by Jack E. Davis.
All rights reserved. Published by Grosset & Dunlap, Inc., a member of Penguin Putnam
Books for Young Readers, New York. THE ZACK FILES is a trademark of The Putnam &
Grosset Group. GROSSET & DUNLAP is a trademark of Grosset & Dunlap, Inc. Published
simultaneously in Canada. Printed in the U.S.A.

Library of Congress Cataloging-in-Publication Data

Greenburg, Dan.
    Never trust a cat who wears earrings / by Dan Greenburg ; illustrated by
Jack E. Davis.
      p. cm.
    Summary: Zack starts turning into a cat when the spirit of an ancient Egyptian cat
goddess is accidentally transferred into his body during a class field trip. [1. Cats–
Fiction. 2. Egypt–Fiction. 3. Supernatural–Fiction.]   I. Davis, Jack E., ill.
II. Title. III. Series: Greenburg, Dan. Zack files.
PZ7.G8278Nj 1997
[Fic]–dc21   96-52899
                                               CIP

2004 Printing
                                               AC

ISBN   0-448-41340-X (pbk.)

Chapter 1

all me Zack. After all, that's my name. So it would be weird to call me anything else. And speaking of weird, I have to admit it. Weird things are always happening to me. So many, in fact, that whenever something normal happens, I almost think it's weird.

I guess I should give you examples of what I'm talking about. Well, my Great-Grandpa Maurice died and came back as a cat, OK? And my friend Spencer and I spent a whole night out of our bodies, flying around Manhattan. And a month ago, I went to get a tooth pulled, and my new orthodontist, Dr. Jekyll, turned into a monster.

Stuff like that.

Anyway, the time I want to tell you about started on a class trip. Oh, did I say I'm in the fifth grade at the Horace Hyde-White School for Boys? Well, I am. That's in New York City, by the way.

Anyhow, our social studies teacher, Mr. Gatkes, took us to the Metropolitan Museum of Art. We'd been studying about Egypt. So we went all through the Egyptian wing. It's great. They even have a real Egyptian temple there. The Temple of Dendur. Egyptian guys in Egypt took it apart, stone by stone, and mailed it to New

York. I don't know whether Egypt paid the postage or *we* did.

I happen to be pretty interested in mummies. So after I saw the temple, I went looking for some mummies. I walked down a hallway and turned in to a small room. Was there a mummy in it? No. But there was a real live woman. She was kneeling on the floor. It was kind of dark. But I thought she might be sick. So I went up to her.

"Excuse me, ma'am," I said. "Are you sick?"

She didn't answer.

I got worried. I went over to help her. She had this very long black hair and sort of cat-like eyes. One was green and one was gray. She looked kind of spacey. And she was babbling.

"Oh, great goddess!" she said. "The time has come! I am ready."

I couldn't see any goddesses.

"Ma'am, are you OK?" I asked.

I tugged at her arm. She had on this heavy gold bracelet with a stone scarab on it. A scarab, in case you haven't studied about Egypt yet, is a kind of beetle.

The lady didn't answer me.

"Oh, goddess," she said. "Your humble servant is here."

Then she closed her eyes. Maybe she just needed a nap. But then she started swaying back and forth. I was scared she was going to fall smack on her face.

I tried to pull her to her feet. She kept repeating stuff about some great goddess. That's when I started wondering if maybe I should slap her face or something. That's

what they always do in movies when people are acting weird and talking to goddesses.

But this lady was sort of scary looking. She was dressed all in black. There was a gold earring in her right ear. And she had a little mustache.

I decided to give it one more try.

"Ma'am, do you need help or what?" I asked.

Just then I heard a hissing sound. I turned to see what it was. Sitting on a pedestal was a big black cat. A big black cat with a gold earring in its right ear. It reached out and scratched my arm.

"Ouch!" I said.

"Fool!" said the woman.

"What?" I said.

"Stupid fool!" said the woman. "You have ruined everything!"

"I was just trying to help you, ma'am," I said. I rubbed my arm where the cat had scratched me.

"Some help," she said. "You ruined everything! *Everything*!"

The cat made a loud hissing sound again. It wasn't a good sound. I decided it was probably time to leave.

"Well, I guess I'll be going now," I said. "Nice to have met you."

I got out of there fast. I ran down the hallway. A minute later I found my class.

"What happened to your arm?" asked Mr. Gatkes.

"A cat scratched me," I said.

"A cat?" said my friend Spencer Sharp. "What cat?"

"A big black one," I said. "With a gold earring."

"They don't allow cats in here," said

Vernon Manteuffel. Vernon is not my friend, even though I did once help him get rid of a ghost in his apartment. But that's a whole other story.

"You want to bet?" I said.

"Sure. I'll bet you a thousand dollars," said Vernon. Vernon is very rich, and he always makes sure you remember that.

"I won't bet you a thousand dollars," I said. "But I'll prove it. C'mon."

I led the class and Mr. Gatkes back to the place where I'd seen the strange lady and the big black cat.

There was nobody there. No big black cat. No babbling lady.

"See?" said Vernon. "There's nobody here. You owe me a thousand dollars."

"They were here just a minute ago," I said. "The cat was right...there."

I pointed to the pedestal. Only now, instead of a real cat, there was a statue of one. It was black but made of smooth stone. And it had the same gold earring in its right ear.

I shook my head. "Two minutes ago that statue was a real cat," I said. "I have the scratch to prove it."

"Oh, right," said Vernon.

"Come, Zack," said Mr. Gatkes. "Let's forget about cats and do something for that scratch."

Mr. Gatkes reached in his backpack and pulled out a first-aid kit. He put some stuff on my arm and a Band-Aid.

"There," he said. "Now that scratch won't trouble you anymore."

Mr. Gatkes didn't know how wrong he was.

Chapter 2

After the museum trip I went home with Spencer. It was a Friday and I was sleeping over at his house.

I just couldn't get what happened at the museum out of my head.

"Spencer," I said, "that cat statue was a real cat when I saw it before. I swear."

Spencer was opening up this kite-making kit he'd bought. He stopped and looked at me seriously.

"Maybe so," he said. "Stranger things have been known to happen."

That's what I like about Spencer. He knows about weird stuff, too. I knew he wouldn't act like I was nuts.

"Lots of strange stuff went on in ancient Egypt," he said. "Maybe we should do some research and see what we turn up."

Did I mention that Spencer is a genius? Well, he is. His IQ is around 1000, I think. He's always doing research on something.

So Spencer got out some books on Egypt for us to look through. We also looked up stuff on his computer. We found out that people in ancient Egypt believed in gods. These gods were part human and part animal. One god looked like a bull. Another one looked like a hawk. There was a goddess named Nut—I swear I'm not making this up. Nut looked like a cow. And then—bingo! We read about a goddess named Bast, who was part cat!

"Look at this!" I shouted. "The weird lady in the museum kept talking about some goddess."

There was a picture of Bast. She had slanty eyes and a gold ring in her right ear, just like the cat that scratched me in the museum. The gold earring was supposed to be a sign of Bast's powers.

"Spencer," I said, "that's just what the cat in the museum looked like."

A shiver went right through me. This was really weird. But just then Spencer's mom called us in to dinner. So I had to forget about the goddess Bast for now.

Dinner was pizza and milk. Normally I love pizza and drink only about half my milk. This time I hardly touched the pizza.

But I kept getting refills of milk. When I was pouring my sixth glass, some milk splashed on the table. Before I could stop myself, I bent over and lapped it up. Mrs. Sharp gave me a funny look.

"Uh, sorry, Mrs. Sharp," I said. "I, uh, just didn't want any milk to go to waste."

Spencer tugged at my arm.

"C'mon, Zack. You're finished eating. Let's go back to my room."

Spencer wanted to find out more about Bast, the cat goddess. But suddenly it didn't seem all that important. I felt really good after drinking all that milk. What I really wanted to do was curl up in a chair and take a nap.

"Well, if you don't want to look up more Egypt stuff," said Spencer, "then let's put my kite together."

I watched Spencer take out the wood,

the tissue paper, and the string. But I had zero interest in putting together his kite. For some reason, all I wanted to do was play with the ball of string. I pawed at it. It unrolled in a very interesting way. I started to swat at it again. But Spencer stopped me.

"Cut it out, Zack," said Spencer. He sounded kind of annoyed.

"Sorry," I said.

I stretched and yawned. I felt really sleepy. Sleepy and peaceful...

The next thing I knew Spencer was shaking me awake. It was morning. I wasn't in bed. I was sleeping on the floor, curled up in a puddle of sunlight. I was still wearing my clothes from the night before.

"C'mon, Zack," said Spencer. "Wake up. You've been asleep since eight o'clock last night."

"I have?" I stretched and yawned and tried to go back to sleep again.

"Yeah," he said. "You fell asleep right on the floor. I tried waking you, but you were out. O-U-T."

Spencer opened the window.

"It's nice and windy today," he said. "I finished the kite. Let's go to the park and fly it."

Normally, I'd love to do that. But today I just wanted to lie around and sleep for a while. Like all day long.

I didn't want to disappoint Spencer, though. So I finally got up and put on some fresh clothes. And we set off for the park. It's a really pretty park, way over by the Hudson River. You can see the Twin Towers of the World Trade Center. Which, in case you don't know, are 110 stories high.

I was so sleepy I could hardly walk. But near the sandbox I saw something that woke me right up.

Birds!

I stopped and stared at them. It was like I'd never seen birds before. They were fascinating. More fascinating than anything. I started to creep up on them.

"C'mon, Zack," said Spencer. "Help me get this kite in the air."

I didn't answer him. I was too busy looking at the birds. I made a funny little clicking sound in my throat. Spencer looked at me strangely.

"Are you OK?" he asked.

I nodded, but I wasn't.

Why was I suddenly so interested in birds? I had never cared about birds. Now all I wanted to do was watch them. Now all I wanted to do was play with them. Now all

I wanted to do was…eat them. The thought made me shudder.

I tried to keep my mind on the kite. But from the corner of my eye I kept watching birds. Especially one nice fat one. It was all I could do to keep myself from pouncing! What was wrong with me?

A few minutes later, Spencer's kite got ripped by a tree branch. So Spencer decided to go back home. And I went to my dad's apartment.

I don't know if I mentioned this before. My parents are divorced. I pretty much divide my time between my mom's place and my dad's.

I was just about to tell Dad about what happened at the museum when I saw him unpacking this humongous box.

"Look what came!" said Dad. "The new TV!"

It was a cool large-screen model. We had picked it out together. Dad was busy reading the instruction booklet.

For weeks I'd been waiting for that TV to arrive. But now, all of a sudden, the box that the TV came in seemed way cooler to me.

"Wow!" I shouted. I jumped into the carton and whirled around inside it. I was having the best time!

Dad peered in at me.

"Zack," he said, "I've got the TV plugged in now. Don't you want to watch the Yankees game with me?"

"Maybe later, Dad," I said. "I'm kind of busy right now."

Dad looked at me with a puzzled expression.

"Do you feel OK?" he asked.

"Actually, I don't," I said. I knew Dad had

only been joking. But I wasn't. "I feel kind of weird," I said. "It all started yesterday. At the museum. A big black cat with a gold earring scratched me."

Now Dad looked worried. He took a look at the scratch.

"You've had your tetanus shots," he said. "So it's not tetanus."

"No," I said, "it's definitely not tetanus."

Dad went to the phone and called my doctor. He told him about the scratch and about how I'd been acting. The doctor didn't think there was anything to worry about.

"Zack is a perfectly normal ten-year-old boy," said the doctor. "They all act a little weird at times."

Dad hung up the phone and went to get the vacuum cleaner to clean up around the new TV. Dad is sort of a neat freak. When he turned on the vacuum, I hid under the coffee table.

Dad turned off the vacuum. He got down on the floor and looked under the coffee table.

"Zack," he said gently. "What are you doing under there?"

"Uh, well, I'm not sure," I said. "I think the vacuum must have spooked me or something."

"I see," said Dad. You could tell he didn't, though.

Suddenly I thought about all the weird stuff I'd been doing—licking up spilled milk, sleeping all curled up on the floor, sneaking up on birds. It all started to make sense.

"Dad," I said in a scared voice. "You know what I think is happening to me?"

"What?" said Dad.

"I think I'm turning into a cat!" I said.

"Oh, right," said Dad. He laughed. But it was a nervous laugh. The kind you laugh when your son tells you he's turning into a cat.

I crawled out from under the coffee table. Dad went into the kitchen to get some glass cleaner. When he came out, I was on the floor next to the sofa.

"Zack," said Dad. "What are you doing now?"

"Well, let's see," I said. "I seem to be sharpening my fingernails on the sofa here." I slumped against the sofa. "I'm sorry, Dad. I really am."

"Zack, what can we do?" he asked.

"I don't know," I said. "Maybe get me a scratching post?"

Dad didn't laugh this time. Not even with

that nervous laugh of his. "OK," said Dad. "That's it. Come on, Zack. Put on your coat."

"Where are we going?" I asked.

"Where we should have gone in the first place."

"Where's that?" I asked.

"To the vet," he said.

Chapter 3

There's a vet about a block from our house. We took my Great-Grandpa Maurice there for a checkup when we found out he'd been reincarnated as a cat.

"Good to see you again," said the vet.

"Thanks for taking us on such short notice," said my dad.

"Well, today's a slow day," said the vet. "Not like tomorrow. The cat show is coming to town. Besides, you said it was an emergency."

"It is," I said.

"Did you bring the little fella?" he asked.

"Of course," said Dad.

"Well, where is he?" said the vet.

"Here," I said.

"Well, bring him into my room," said the vet. "We'll have a look at him."

"He's already in here," said my dad.

"Where?" said the vet. He looked under the examination table.

"Right here," I said. I pointed to myself.

"I thought you had a sick cat," said the vet.

"No," said Dad. "I have a sick boy who's turning *into* a cat."

The vet started laughing.

"You know, I thought I'd heard them all," he said. "But that's a new one on me!"

"This isn't a joke," I said. "I really am turning into a cat. I want to eat birds. I hide when I hear a vacuum cleaner. I sharpen my nails on the sofa. OK?"

The vet looked at Dad. Then he looked at me.

"You're serious about this?" he asked us.

Dad nodded.

The vet shrugged and threw up his hands.

"Well," he said to me. "Hop up on the table. Let's have a look at you."

I hopped up on the table. The vet began to examine me. At first he didn't seem concerned at all. He flashed a light in my eyes. He looked inside my ears. He made some notes on a clipboard. There was a slightly puzzled look on his face.

"This all started yesterday at the museum," I said. "A big black cat scratched me. I think that has something to do with my turning into a cat."

"Nonsense," said the vet. "I get scratched all the time. You don't see me hiding when I hear a vacuum cleaner."

"But I bet you were never scratched by a cat that turned into a statue," I said.

He was listening to my heart now. He thumped me on the chest a couple of times. Then he listened to my heart again. His face was more serious now. He took a look inside my mouth with his flashlight. Except he didn't ask me to open it. He just opened it himself.

"Good boy," he said as he peered inside my mouth. Then he made some more notes and scratched me under the chin.

"This is a most interesting case. Could you leave him here overnight for observation?" the vet asked Dad. He patted me on the back. "I'd like to keep my eye on the little fella. Just to be on the safe side."

I realized the vet wasn't talking to me anymore. He was talking only to my dad.

"You most certainly cannot keep him overnight for observation," said Dad.

"Why not?" said the vet.

"Zack is a boy, not a cat," said Dad.

The vet shrugged.

"Suit yourself," he said. "He's probably due for some shots, though."

This was too much!

"I don't want any shots!" I said. "Especially not ones for cats!"

"He won't even feel it," said the vet, as if I couldn't understand him. "They don't, you know."

Dad got me out of there fast. As soon as we were outside, I felt better.

Then a lady passed us with a cocker spaniel on a leash. I arched my back and hissed at it.

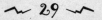

Chapter 4

"I just wish I knew what to do for you," Dad said. "That vet was no help at all."

I sighed. Only it came out sort of like a meow. Then I thought that maybe there was one person—well, not a person exactly—who might be able to help me.

My Great-Grandpa Maurice. The one who died and came back as a cat. He was living in Florida now. Maurice obviously knew about turning from a person into a cat.

Maybe he also knew about turning from a cat back into a person.

"Dad," I said, "why don't we go to Florida and see Great-Grandpa Maurice? I bet he'd know what to do."

"We can't afford to go to Florida," said Dad. "But we can certainly call him."

Dad found Maurice's phone number in Palm Beach. I dialed it. It took a while for the lady who answered to get Maurice to come to the phone. "Poopsie pie, it's for you!" she kept shouting. At last Maurice was on the line.

"Great-Grandpa Maurice," I said. "It's Zack. How are you doing?"

"Zack!" said Maurice. "I haven't heard from you in a dog's age! How the heck are you?"

"OK," I said. "Well, not so OK, if you

want to know the truth. Which is the main reason I'm calling."

"What's wrong, kid?" Maurice asked. He sounded worried.

"Is that Zack?" called the lady who'd answered the phone. "Tell him hello! Tell him I can't wait to meet him!"

"Listen," I said, "I'm really worried. I've been acting kind of strange."

"Bernice," Maurice called to the lady. "Be a doll and fix me a little herring and sour cream." Then he returned to our conversation. "Don't worry, Zack," he said. "I'm sure you'll be your old self again in a day or so."

"No, I won't," I said.

"What do you mean?"

"My old self was a boy," I said. "But I seem to be turning into a cat."

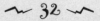

There was a pause on the other end of the line.

"Run that past me again, would you, Zack?"

"I said I'm turning into a cat."

"What makes you think so?"

So I told Maurice every weird cat-like thing that I'd been doing.

"All perfectly normal," said Maurice. "I do all of those things myself."

"But you *are* a cat," I said.

"Mmmmmm," he said. "Good point. Well, maybe you are turning into a cat. But so what?"

I couldn't believe he said that.

"Don't you care?" I asked him.

"Of course I care," he said. "I'm your great-grandfather. But I'm also a cat. And, frankly, it's not such a bad life. You lie around in the sun all day. At night they feed you and scratch your belly. Is that bad? I ask you. Listen, when you've completely turned into a cat, we can hang out together. We'll watch birds. We'll take naps. For laughs we'll chase our tails."

"All right!" I said. Then I stared at the phone. What was I saying? "No! I don't want this to happen to me!"

There was another pause.

"Listen, kid," said Maurice. "I know you must be upset. And I want to help you. I happen to be flying up to New York tomorrow for the cat show. Come and see me. I'll be there all day. It's at Madison Square Garden. Booth 87. Will you do that?"

I sighed. "I guess so," I said. Then I hung up the phone.

"Well," said Dad. "What did Maurice say?"

"I'll tell you as soon as I go to the bathroom," I said. I walked into the bathroom. Then I walked out again.

"Uh, Dad," I said, "is there any chance we have a litter box around somewhere?"

Chapter 5

The next morning I went to the bathroom to brush my teeth. I was half asleep. But when I looked into the medicine-cabinet mirror, I woke up fast.

I had whiskers!

"Dad!" I yelled. "Dad, come in here! Fast!"

My voice sounded weird. Halfway between talking and meowing.

Dad came racing into the bathroom.

"What's wrong?" he asked. "Are you all right?"

"Look," I said. I pointed to my face.

He leaned over and squinted.

"Well," he said, "I knew you'd grow whiskers someday, Zack. I just didn't expect them so soon. Or in neat rows on both sides of your nose."

Dad came back with his electric razor.

"I sure hope Maurice can help us," he said.

Then he plugged in the razor and gave me my first shave.

The cat show was amazing. There were hundreds of cats in Madison Square Garden. Thousands of cats. Siamese cats. Persian cats. Himalayan cats. Abyssinian cats. Manx cats. Rex cats. Russian Blues, which are actually not blue but gray. Each one was next to its proud owner.

There were cats with really long, bushy fur. There were cats without any fur at all. The hairless cats looked wrinkly and gross. They looked like they needed to be ironed or something.

People in booths were selling all kinds of cat stuff. Cat collars. Cat brushes. Cat toys. I begged Dad to buy me a rubber mouse, but he said no.

There was a little roped-off area where judges were looking over cats. Lifting their paws. Lifting them into a standing position. Lifting their tails. None of these cats seemed to be having any fun.

When we got to Booth 87, there was Great-Grandpa Maurice. I almost didn't recognize him. He looked like a brand-new

cat. Last time I saw him he was a scruffy old gray tomcat. Last time I saw him he was missing half the whiskers on the left side of his face.

Now he was clean, fluffed up, and really well groomed. And his whiskers had grown back in, or else he was wearing fake ones. But it was Maurice all right. He was sneaking puffs on a big cigar. I guess the judges had a thing about cats smoking.

A lady about the same age as my Grandma Leah was holding his cigar and fussing over him. You could tell she was crazy about him.

I went right over and hugged him.

"Zack!" Maurice said in a low voice. "You came!"

He looked around quickly. I guess to make sure no one could hear a cat talking.

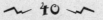

"Zack, Dan—say hello to Bernice," said Maurice. "It was her idea to enter me in this show. Bernice, this is my great-grand-son, Zack. And my grandson, Dan."

"Maurice has told me a lot about both of you," said Bernice.

"I met this lovely lady in a deli in Palm Beach," Maurice explained. "We were both buying pickles. Kosher dills. It was love at first sight."

Bernice seemed very nice. She was kind of plump. She was wearing a very large dress with flowers all over it. Spencer and I could have used it for a tent. She also had really big hair that didn't move. The color of her hair was one I had never seen before.

"So, Maurice," said Dad. "Do you have any ideas about how to help Zack?"

"I don't know," said Maurice. "How's your condition, Zack? Any better?"

"No," I said. "Worse."

"Don't look so sad, both of you," said Maurice. "Hey, here's a cat joke to cheer you up: What kind of car do cats drive in Florida?"

"I don't know," I said. "But I'm not really in the mood for jokes right now."

"A Catillac," said Maurice. "A *Cat*-illac. Get it?"

"Yeah," I said, "I get it. Have you thought about my problem at all?"

"Sure, sure," he said. "But first we have to cheer you up. OK, another joke: What two sports cars do cats like best?"

"Come on, I already told you I'm not in the mood for jokes," I said.

"A Furrari and a Mousarati," said

Maurice, chuckling. He poked Bernice in the ribs. "A *Fur*-rari and a *Mouse*-arati," he said. "Get it?"

Bernice giggled and hugged him.

"Maurice," said Dad. "Zack and I are really worried. This morning he discovered whiskers. And if you look closely, his ears are getting kind of pointy."

"What?" I shouted. "They are?"

"I didn't want to alarm you," said Dad.

"Great-Grandpa Maurice, are you going to help me or not?" I asked. "Because if you aren't..."

All at once I stopped talking. Right then I caught sight of somebody I never expected to see again. It was the weird lady from the museum!

Chapter 6

The weird lady from the museum was sitting in a booth. She had all kinds of gifts for sale. Cat key rings. Cat mugs. Cat sweaters. Cat earmuffs. Bumper stickers that said: CATS RULE. There were even little gold statues of the cat goddess Bast. Each one had a tiny gold earring in one ear.

"Excuse me, ma'am," I called out. "I have to talk to you!" I started for her booth.

"Where are you going?" asked Dad.

"It's the cat lady from the museum," I said. When I got to her booth, she looked up at me with those weird two-color eyes.

"It's you!" she cried.

"Yes, it's me," I said. "What's happening? Your cat scratched me in the museum. And now I'm turning into a cat myself!"

"What happened to you was a mistake," she hissed at me. "That honor was supposed to be mine."

"Honor?" I said. "Being turned into a cat is an honor?"

"Yes, of course it is an honor to have the spirit of the Great Cat Goddess Bast enter one's body and transform it."

"Yikes!" I said. "Is that what's happening to me? The spirit of Bast has entered my body?"

She nodded seriously. "According to the

prophecy, this honor is given once every thousand years to a member of the royal family. Not to some...some ordinary child."

The way she said "child" made it sound like a dirty word.

"I was the chosen one," she said. "You see, I am her royal highness, Princess Katima." She acted like I was supposed to bow down to her or something.

"And all this happened when I got scratched?" I asked.

Another nod.

"At the exact moment I was to get the sacred scratch, you stepped in the way."

"Hey, I'm sorry, all right?"

"Foolish boy!" she cried. "I have been waiting for years! Years! Instead you will be transformed by the Great Cat Goddess Bast. And I will be...chopped liver!"

"You know," I said, "I'm not exactly thrilled about the sacred-scratch mix-up either. I'm planning to become a major league baseball player when I grow up. That's going to be hard enough to do as a person. I don't even want to think how hard it would be as a cat. Look, isn't there anything we can do?"

"What do you mean?"

"Well, you were mentioning some prophecy," I said. "Didn't it say anything about what to do if somebody messes up?"

"Of course," she said. "But there is no way to correct such a mistake. Not here in this country." The lady then picked up one of the books she was selling. I could see that the pages were all in hieroglyphics. She began to read:

"'In the year of the Papyrus'—that is the current year—'the spirit of the Goddess

Bast shall pass into the body of the one who has one green eye and one gray one...."

"But I don't have one green eye and one gray one," I broke in.

"That is why you are a mistake!" shouted Princess Katima. "A blooper! A screwup in the cosmic clockwork of the universe!"

"I said I was sorry about that," I replied.

Princess Katima gave me a disgusted look and started reading again.

"'Should a mishap occur, there will be a forty-eight-hour grace period to correct it. In the hour between light and darkness, on the banks of the Great River, in the shadow of the stones that touch the clouds, gather a handful of sand from where you stand and fling it into the wind. As the last grain of sand falls to the ground, you shall scratch the right and true heir.'"

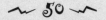

She closed the book.

"'The Great River,'" she said, "is the Nile, of course. And 'the stones that touch the clouds' are the tips of the Great Pyramids. But the Nile and the pyramids are in Egypt. And the forty-eight-hour period is almost up. We could never get to Egypt in time. So to correct the mishap is quite impossible, you see."

Well, maybe it was OK with the princess here if I became a cat. But it sure wasn't OK with me. There had to be a way out. I tried to think like Spencer.

"Does the prophecy actually say it has to be the Nile?" I asked.

"Well, no....Not exactly," she said. "Why?"

"Because New York happens to have some pretty great rivers, too. Like the Hudson."

The minute I said "Hudson," it was like little flashbulbs went off—pop!—in my head. I remembered the park by Spencer's house. And how you could see the Twin Towers of the World Trade Center.

"I fail to see how the Hud—"

I didn't let the princess finish. "Listen," I said. "My friend Spencer lives near a park that's right on the Hudson. It's near the Twin Towers, which also happen to have a lot of 'stones that touch the clouds.' The park even has a sandbox."

"So...?"

"So, maybe we can fix the mistake without going all the way to Egypt."

"It will never work," she said.

Boy, I wondered if everybody in the royal family was that negative.

"Look, Princess," I said. "It's our only hope. So let's get going!"

Chapter 7

"**W**e're going *where* to do *what*?" said Dad. He looked pretty upset. I was pulling him by the arm.

"We're going to Spencer's park. To try and undo this prophecy. I'll tell you all about it later, Dad, believe me. This is my one chance to become a boy again!"

We said quick good-byes to Maurice and Bernice.

Then we rushed out of Madison Square

Garden—Dad, the princess, and me. We hopped in a cab.

By the time we got to Spencer's park, the sun was sinking into the river. Yikes! Just a few minutes between life as a normal boy and eating Meow Mix every day for breakfast.

It took me a minute to find the sandbox. Two little kids were building a castle together.

"Shoo, small children! Scat!" shouted Princess Katima.

They scatted. We got into the sandbox. Katima started swaying back and forth, waving her arms over her head. Dad and I had to sway, too. Then Katima faced the river and began to chant. I couldn't understand the words, so it must have been in a foreign language. Egyptian or Pig Latin or something.

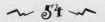

"Repeat after me!" said Princess Katima. I tried my best. But I had no idea what I was saying.

About halfway through the chant, Spencer wandered by, carrying his kite.

"Hey, Zack," he cried. "What the heck are you doing here?"

"Shhhhhh!" I said. I kept on swaying, but I stopped waving my arms. I pointed to the princess.

"What's going on?" he asked. "Who's she? And, hey, how come your ears are so pointy?"

I clapped my hand over his mouth.

"I was turning into a cat," I whispered. "But the princess here is trying to fix that. You're just in time to help. Join us in the chanting. Repeat everything she says."

So now there were four of us chanting and swaying. Then suddenly the princess stopped and looked at me. The sun was about to plop right into New Jersey.

I picked up a handful of sand and threw it in the air. As the last grain fell to the ground, I scratched the princess on the arm.

I looked into her face. I swear, for a split second I saw the face of Bast the cat goddess, too. It was like a photo that gets double-exposed or something.

"What do we do now?" I asked.

"Now?" she said. "Now?"

"Yes, now," I said.

Her face had gotten this incredibly happy expression on it.

"Now?" she repeated. "Mow?"

"What?" I said.

"Mow?" she said. "Meow?"

A strange noise was coming from her throat. She was purring!

Chapter 8

Suddenly I felt a tingling on my face. I reached up. What do you know? My whiskers were gone! I touched my ears. They weren't pointy anymore! I thought about birds. Blue jays. Yellow canaries. Red cardinals with tufts on their heads. Tiny hummingbirds. I found the idea of birds really, really...boring.

As soon as Dad and I got home, I phoned Great-Grandpa Maurice at his hotel. I told

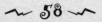

What else happens to Zack?
Find out in

*My Son,
the Time Traveler*

Grandma Leah swiveled her chair around.

"This is a lovely young man, Zack," she said, facing Mack. "Is he a friend from school?"

"Uh, not exactly," I said.

"Then how do you know him, dear?"

I looked at Mack. He shrugged. Grandma Leah is eighty-eight, but she's a very peppy, open-minded person. I was sure she'd be able to handle hearing who Mack was.

"Grandma," I said, "Mack is my son."

him I'd stopped turning into a cat. I told him I was a boy again.

"Great news, Zack!" said Maurice. "Hey, I got news of my own!"

"What's that?" I asked.

"I won a second-place ribbon! For Best Domestic Shorthair in the Senior Division!"

So there was a happy ending for everybody! I'm really glad to be a boy again. I don't play with string anymore. I don't hiss at dogs. I have no use for a litter box. I don't sharpen my nails on the sofa. I've completely lost my interest in birds. But when my dad uses the vacuum cleaner, I still do hide under the coffee table.

Oh well, five out of six isn't bad.